# The cat

# that became

# a Unicorn

Anita V. Sanders

Aphrodite Editions

**Content:**

# Chapter 1

# The stray cat

In a bustling alley in the city, among flashes of neon lights and the echo of hurried footsteps, lived a stray cat named Simon. He was a white-furred feline with bright yellow eyes that flashed with cunning and curiosity. He spent his days wandering the narrow streets, searching for food among market scraps, and sleeping under the stars.

Despite his difficult life, Simón kept a spark of joy in his heart. He loved watching humans pass by, imagining the stories behind each face and hurried step. He dreamed of adventures beyond the confines of the alley and wondered if one day he could find his own special destiny.

One afternoon, while he was wandering around the market looking for something to eat, Simon heard a rustling in the wind. It was a soft and mysterious murmur that seemed to call him from the depths of his being. Intrigued, he followed the sound until he reached a dark corner where he found an old owl perched on a branch.

"Who are you?" Simon asked, feeling a mix of curiosity and fear.

The owl turned her head gracefully and responded with a wise and serene voice: "I am the keeper of ancient secrets, the guide of those who seek their destiny. I have sensed your restlessness, young cat, and I am here to offer you a path to true greatness."

Simon gasped at the owl's words. Never before had he encountered someone so mysterious and fascinating. With his heart beating with excitement, he decided to follow the owl and discover what fate awaited him.

Thus began the adventure of Simón, the stray cat, in search of his true purpose in the world.

# Chapter 2

## The mysterious call

Following the old owl through the dark alley, Simon became more and more intrigued by the mysterious call that resonated inside him. The owl, with its silent and elegant flight, seemed to lead him towards an unknown and intriguing, but... exciting destination.

The alley took them to the outskirts of the city, where tall, noisy buildings gave way to open fields and tree-lined paths. Simon marveled at the tranquil beauty of nature and the fresh air that filled his lungs.

"Where are you taking me?" Simon asked the owl, whose eyes shone with a mysterious light.

"I am taking you towards your destiny, young Simon," replied the feathered bird, in an enigmatic tone. "You have been called by forces beyond your understanding, and it is time for you to discover your true potential."

With every step he took, Simón felt that he was getting closer to the answer he so longed for. The mysterious calling inside him intensified, filling him with a sense of urgency and excitement.

Finally, they reached a clearing in the forest where a rainbow shone in the sky, bathing the landscape in pulsating, bright colors. In the center of the clearing, there was a pool of crystal clear water that reflected the light of the afternoon sun.

"This is the place where your true journey begins," the owl announced solemnly. "Enter the sacred waters and discover your destiny."

Simon looked towards the well determinedly, feeling a mixture of nervousness and excitement. He knew that a great adventure awaited him as he immersed himself in the magical waters of the clearing.

With one last glance at the owl that had guided him there, Simon stepped into the shimmering waters, ready to discover the purpose that had called him from the depths of his being.

Mystery and excitement filled the young cat's heart as he dove into the crystal clear waters, ready to embark on the journey of a lifetime.

And so began the most amazing story that a kitten could have dreamed of.

# Chapter 3
## The revelation

After immersing himself in the sacred waters of the clearing, Simon emerged with a renewed sense of energy and determination. His fur shone in the glare of the sun, and his eyes glinted with a new light. He knew in that moment that something had changed, that he would no longer be the same hapless alley cat, and that he had begun an adventure that would take him beyond anything he imagined.

As he explored the clearing, a shadow fell over him. He looked up and saw the owl, watching him with piercing eyes from a nearby branch.

"You have emerged from the water as a new being," said the owl in his deep, melodic voice. "Now is the time for you to discover your true destiny."

Simon approached her with reverence, feeling deep respect for this wise creature, who had guided him there.

"What is my destiny?" Simon asked anxiously, wanting to know the answer to the question that had driven him from the beginning.

The owl spread its majestic wings and spoke solemnly: "You, Simon, are destined to become the guardian of magic, which for centuries has manifested itself in the form of a "unicorn cat", a unique being that will bring light and hope to the world. But to achieve it, you must embark on a journey full of challenges and discover your hidden abilities."

Simón listened carefully to the owl's words, feeling a mixture of excitement and determination beginning to grow inside him. He knew that this was just the beginning of a great adventure that would take him to unimaginable places.

With a firm nod, Simon said goodbye to the wise owl and headed into the forest, ready to face what the future had in store for him.

Thus, with the call of destiny resounding in his heart, Simón embarked on the next stage of the journey to become the legendary unicorn cat, a guardian of magic and hope in a world full of wonders and challenges.

And so concluded this third chapter of the story of Simon the stray cat, on his path to greatness as the mysterious unicorn cat!

# Chapter 4

# The search

# of the inner treasure

With the owl's words echoing in his mind, Simon headed into the thick forest with determination. He knew that to become the legendary unicorn cat, he must discover his unique abilities and unlock his true potential.

The forest was a labyrinth of winding paths and ancient trees that whispered secrets in the wind. Simón walked with a determined step, eyes and ears wide open, looking for clues about his fate.

Soon, he reached a clearing where he encountered a series of challenges blocking his path. There was a rushing river roaring with fury, a fallen tree blocked the way, and a dark cave emanated a mysterious aura.

Without hesitation, Simón faced each challenge with courage and determination. Using his feline cunning and agility, he crossed the river dexterously, negotiated the fallen tree with ingenuity, and explored the dark cave with courage.

In his search for inner treasure, Simón encountered challenges that tested his skills and ingenuity. But with each one overcome, he came one step closer to discovering his true potential.

Finally, after surpassing them all, Simon arrived at a sunlit clearing, where he found a glowing stone that emitted magical light. With an excited flutter in his chest, he picked up the stone and felt a surge of energy course through his body.

"This is the treasure you've been looking for," said a soft voice in his mind. "It is the power that lies within you, waiting to be used."

Having the stone in his possession, Simon knew that he had taken an important step in his journey to greatness. With renewed determination, he prepared to face the challenges that still awaited him, knowing he had the inner power necessary to triumph.

# Chapter 5

## The test of courage

Having found the inner treasure in the form of the shining stone, Simon continued his journey with renewed boldness. He knew that challenges still awaited him that would test his bravery and determination on the path to becoming the legendary unicorn cat.

As he advanced through the forest, he encountered a group of magical creatures blocking his path. There were huge, hairy trolls that snarled ferociously, and cunning goblins that lurked in the shadows with malice.

Without hesitation, Simón faced them with courage, remembering the lessons of humility and empathy that he had learned on his journey so far. Instead of resorting to violence, he used his cunning and ingenuity to resolve conflicts and find peaceful solutions.

He knew, from others who had told him, that it was of no use to escape or fight the creatures of the forest, because they are powerful; Therefore, when facing the trolls, Simón used his charm and charisma to calm their spirits and convince them to allow him to pass. In turn, with the goblins, he used his intelligence and skill in dialogue to negotiate an agreement that would benefit both parties.

As he overcame each challenge with courage and determination, he felt his heart fill with a sense of purpose and fulfillment. He knew that he was proving his worth as the future guardian of magic and hope, simply because with peace and sympathy he was accomplishing things that others, with violence, had failed to do.

In the end, after passing all the tests successfully, the cat reached a clearing in the forest where he found a magical water fountain that shone with resplendent light. As he drank the crystalline liquid, he felt renewed energy flow through him, strengthening his spirit.

With a heart full of gratitude and hope, Simón prepared to continue his journey toward greatness, knowing that each difficulty overcome brought him one step closer to his destiny as the legendary unicorn cat.

# Chapter 6

# The magical awakening

After passing the test of courage in the enchanted forest, Simon continued his journey with renewed determination. He knew that every test passed had his reward, and that sometimes it is not a toy or food, but simply the satisfaction of having triumphed for oneself.

As he walked along the path, a bright light appeared before him, drawing him toward a sunlit clearing. In the center, there was a majestic century-old tree, whose branches swayed gently in the breeze.

As he approached, the white cat felt a magical presence enveloping him, filling him with a sense of awe and reverence. Then, a soft and melodious voice echoed in his mind.

"Simon, you have shown bravery and determination on your journey so far," the voice said. "The time has come for you to awaken your true power and discover your destiny as the unicorn cat."

With an excited heartbeat, Simón concentrated inside him and opened his heart to the magic that surrounded him. A warm, comforting feeling enveloped him and he slowly began to transform.

His white fur shone with golden light, while majestic brightly colored manes grew on his head. A gleaming horn emerged from his forehead, glinting with the magic that flowed through it.

Finally, Simon opened his eyes and found himself looking at his reflection in a nearby pond. He was no longer a simple stray cat, now he was a majestic unicorn cat, imbued with the magic and power of the ancestors.

With tears of joy in his eyes, he realized that his transformation was not only physical, but also spiritual. He had found the true inner self and embraced his destiny with courage and determination.

With a meow of joy, Simon said goodbye to the enchanted clearing and prepared to share its light and magic with the world. He knew that the journey was not over yet, but he was ready to face any challenge that came his way.

# Chapter 7

## The temptation of power

Turned into the majestic unicorn cat, Simón felt possessed of new strength and wisdom. His fur shone with a golden light as he walked gracefully through the forest paths, aware of his destiny as a guardian of magic and hope.

However, as he progressed on his journey, he found himself facing a powerful temptation: the lure of power and fame. Creatures from everywhere marveled at his presence, admiring his beauty and magical abilities.

At first, Simón was flattered by the attention and respect he received. He enjoyed the adoration of those around him, fueling his pride and sense of importance.

But soon, he began to realize that attention and recognition were not enough to satisfy his soul. As he became more immersed in the pursuit of power and fame, he began to lose sight of what really mattered: his purpose as a guardian of magic and hope.

His actions became selfish and arrogant, and he began to use magic for personal gain instead of helping others. He forgot the lessons of humility and empathy that he had learned on his journey, allowing himself to be carried away by the seduction of power.

But fortunately, the wisdom of the owl and the magic of the enchanted clearing called him back to his true path.

Simón recognized his mistake and repented, simply because at all times he had only thought about himself and not the others. With renewed humility and determination, Simon renounced the temptation of power and pledged to use its magic for the good of all. He realized that his true purpose was to be a beacon of hope and light in a world full of darkness and hopelessness.

# Chapter 8

## The lesson in humility

After giving up the temptation of power and fame, Simon the Unicorn Cat embarked on an inner quest to find the true essence of who he is. He knew that, to fulfill his destiny as a guardian of magic and hope, he needed to continue growing, because no one knows everything, and there is always room for more knowledge. Above all, he needed to cultivate humility and empathy in his heart.

On the journey, he encountered creatures of all shapes and sizes, each with their own stories and challenges.

As he listened to his stories and shared experiences, he began to understand the importance of walking in the shoes of others and showing compassion toward those who were suffering.

One afternoon, while exploring a quiet valley, Simon came across a family of rabbits struggling to find food for their babies. Without hesitation, Simon offered help, using his magic to create a fertile field full of delicious vegetables and fruits.

The rabbits looked at him with gratitude and amazement, grateful for his generosity and kindness. He smiled humbly, feeling a deep connection with the creatures he had helped.

As he continued his journey, Simon found more opportunities to show humility and empathy toward those in need. He no longer sought attention or recognition, but instead found satisfaction in the simple act of doing good and helping others. He always said to himself, "If I can make someone else smile, I will be happy."

With each act of kindness, he felt his heart fill with light. He had learned the most important lesson of all: that true greatness lies in selfless service and compassion toward others.

# Chapter 9

# The return home

Having learned important lessons in humility and empathy on the journey, Simon the unicorn cat was filled with gratitude and determination. He knew that he had found his true purpose as a guardian of magic and hope, and he was ready to share his light with the world.

With his heart overflowing with love and compassion, Simón decided to return to the place where it all began: his home in the city alley. Despite the adversities and challenges faced on the journey, he never forgot where he came from or the creatures that shared his life in the alley.

Upon arrival, Simon met his old friends: stray cats, stray dogs and songbirds. He greeted them warmly and told them about his journey and the lessons he had learned along the way.

Upon hearing the stories, the creatures in the alley first laughed and doubted, but when they touched the horn that Simon had on his forehead, and realized it was true, they believed him. Then they felt inspired and encouraged. They began to see the world with new eyes and find hope in the midst of darkness.

The cat became a symbol of hope and kindness to all who knew him, and his home in the alley a haven of love and compassion.

Over time, stories about the unicorn cat spread beyond this corner of the city and reached the ears of creatures everywhere. Simón became a living legend, a symbol of courage and determination for all those who longed for a better world.

But despite his fame and recognition, he never forgot his roots nor stopped being the same humble and compassionate cat he always was. He continued to share his light with the world and help those in need, reminding them that true greatness lies in the heart.

# Chapter 10

## The legacy of the unicorn cat

As time passed, Simon the Unicorn Cat continued to spread his message of love and compassion around the world, leaving a legacy of hope and kindness. The story became a beloved tale for creatures everywhere, inspiring future generations to follow in its footsteps.

In the alley where it all began, a statue was erected in honor of Simón, remembering his bravery and dedication to making the world a better place. The creatures of the alley gathered around the statue to tell their stories and remember the unconditional love for all those around him.

In every city or village in the world, the people and creatures who had been touched by Simon's magic carried the legacy with them, sharing the message of hope and gratitude with those around them. Each person and each creature that put Simon's teachings into practice was spiritually transformed into a unicorn cat, as they remembered the value of peace and effort, which, even in the darkest moments, allow one to find light and power in oneself.

Over time, the world became a kinder and more compassionate place, where all creatures could live in harmony and bliss. And although Simon no longer physically walked among them, his spirit lived on in every act of kindness and gesture of compassion, reminding them that love is the most powerful force of all.

And so concluded the story of Simon the unicorn cat, whose legacy would live on forever in the hearts of those who had been touched by his light. His life was a reminder that even the humblest of beings can bring hope and transformation to the world, simply by sharing love and compassion with others.

**Moral:** "True magic lies in the courage to be yourself and the power to help others discover their own inner light."

# The mystery of the

# silenced song

In a small town surrounded by mountains, there lived a detective owl named Bruno. He was known for his keen hearing and his ability to decipher the faintest sounds.

It is said that he once managed to discover who was stealing Mr. Rabbit's carrots, and that it turned out to be himself, who woke up asleep (they call him a sleepwalker) and ate them. On another occasion he knew how to find the house keys for Mr. Hippopotamus, who couldn't see them, because his big belly hid them from him.

But this story focuses on the time a sad swallow came to ask for help.

"Mr. Bruno!" sobbed the swallow, "I have lost my song. I can no longer cheer the people with my melody." Bruno, with her understanding look, told her: "Do not worry, swallow, I will help you find your song."

But how will he achieve it, if the song is invisible? said the feathered bird.

Don't worry, the owl responded, not everything we don't see is non-existent. For example, love is not seen, but it is felt.

Bruno walked through the town, listening carefully to every sound.

Lying on the sidewalk he saw a dog that was barking and wagging its tail. It didn't seem to him that that was the lost voice of the swallow. The same thing happened with the meowing of a cat on the roof, which was asking for food; and even less so with the neighing of a horse that he was happy because his owner was taking him out for a walk.

He was practically giving up, because that voice was elusive. Bruno had given her word to the swallow and that gave him strength, because he did not want to let her down. That's why he insisted, since he wanted to see the swallow happy.

From walking and searching so much, he heard a familiar song coming from a golden cage in the mayor's house. When she looked out, she saw a caged canary that was singing sadly.

Bruno came up with a plan. He went to the mayor's house and, pretending to be a bird seller, offered him an exchange: a voice-imitating parrot for the canary. The mayor, fascinated by the idea of having a bird that imitated sounds, accepted the deal.

Bruno freed the canary and took him to the town square. The swallow, upon seeing it, was filled with joy and together they sang a beautiful song that filled all the inhabitants with joy.

**Moral:** Freedom is essential for creativity. You cannot force someone to express themselves if they are not in an environment where they feel free and happy. True beauty lies in the authenticity of each being.

Other children's literary works by the author
that you will find on this platform:

• How to become a real life fairy

• The Wise Giraffe

• The challenges of being a mother